THOMAS & FRIENDS

The Adventure Begins

Adapted from the original screenplay by Andrew Brenner

A Random House PICTUREBACK® Book

Random House New York

Thomas the Tank Engine & Friends™

CREATED BY BRITT ALLCROFT

Based on The Railway Series by The Reverend W Awdry.
© 2015 Gullane (Thomas) LLC.
Thomas the Tank Engine & Friends and Thomas & Friends are trademarks of Gullane (Thomas) Limited.
HIT and the HIT Entertainment logo are trademarks of HIT Entertainment Limited.
All rights reserved. Published in the United States by Random House Children's Books, a division of Random House LLC, 1745 Broadway,
New York, NY 10019, and in Canada by Random House of Canada Limited, Toronto, Penguin Random House Companies. Pictureback,
Random House, and the Random House colophon are registered trademarks of Random House LLC.

ISBN 978-0-553-53553-2 (trade) — ISBN 978-0-553-53552-5 (ebook)

randomhousekids.com   www.thomasandfriends.com

Printed in the United States of America   10 9 8 7 6 5 4 3 2 1

A long time ago on the Island of Sodor, there was a little railway known as the North Western. Sir Topham Hatt was in charge.

Many engines worked on the railway. The biggest, Gordon, pulled the Express. The smallest, Edward, shunted trucks and coaches for the bigger engines. James had wooden brake blocks that sometimes smoked when he stopped.

One day, Gordon told the others that a new engine was coming to the railway. "The last one we got was too small to be Really Useful," he said unkindly.

"I'm not *small*!" declared James.

The new engine's name was Thomas. He had six small wheels; a short, stumpy funnel; a short, stumpy boiler; and a short, stumpy dome.

Thomas seemed awfully small.

"Sir Topham Hatt must have made a mistake if he was expecting someone Really Useful," Gordon said.

"I *am* Really Useful!" cried Thomas.

Thomas tried hard to be Really Useful. At first, he made a lot of mistakes.

He huffed and puffed and rushed to and fro. He biffed and bashed into trucks and got in Gordon's way.

"Oh, that's very useful, isn't it?" Gordon snorted.

Thomas' first day on the railway hadn't gone well, but he felt sure he'd soon get the hang of things.

The cheeky little engine spotted Gordon asleep in a siding. He crept up and blew his whistle.

"Wake up, lazybones!" Thomas shouted. "Why don't you work hard like me?"

Thomas hurried off, laughing. Gordon was quite cross with Thomas.

One rainy night in the Sheds, Thomas met Henry, who looked worried.
"Henry doesn't like rain," Edward explained. He told Thomas Henry's story.
"Once an engine attached to a train was afraid of a few drops of rain. It rushed
into a tunnel and squeaked through its funnel and never came out again!"

"Henry wouldn't budge," continued Edward. "He said the rain would spoil his lovely green paint and red stripes. He refused to move, even after the rain stopped. In the end, Henry had to be pulled out of the tunnel with a rope. That's why he's afraid of rain."

One morning, Sir Topham Hatt sent Thomas to the Steamworks
to be repainted in the colors he liked to see on his railway.
A man painted Thomas' water tank and dome blue.
Another trimmed his windows with yellow paint.

One used red paint to add stripes.

Another man carefully marked out the number 1 on his side.

Thomas raced proudly back into the Yard. "Look, Edward, I'm blue, just like you!"

Edward laughed happily. "You're also number 1."

"That means I'm the best!" cried Thomas.

The next morning, Thomas had to fetch Gordon's Express coaches. But he arrived late.

"Hurry up, you!" Gordon scowled impatiently.

"Hurry up, yourself!" Thomas retorted.

Gordon decided to teach Thomas a lesson.

Gordon pulled away very quickly. There was no time to uncouple
Thomas from the coaches. Gordon dragged Thomas along behind him
and raced around a bend.

"Stop! Stop!" cried Thomas.

"Hurry! Hurry! Hurry!" Gordon said with a grin. And on he raced.

At last, Gordon pulled into a station.
"Well, little Thomas, now you know what hard work is like!" he called.

Poor Thomas puffed slowly away to rest. He had a long drink from the water tower. "I want to pull my own train," he complained. "I want to see the world!"

One day, Henry couldn't work. Sir Topham Hatt asked Thomas to pull Henry's coaches.

At the station, Sir Topham Hatt warned Thomas to wait until everything was ready. But Thomas was too excited. He raced off before the coaches were coupled up!

"Thomas! Stop! Come back!" shouted Sir Topham Hatt. Thomas didn't even hear him.

"I'm doing it! I'm pulling a train!" Thomas said happily as he raced along the line. "Everyone says it's hard to pull trains, but *I* think it's easy."

Then Thomas saw a red signal ahead and slowed to a stop.

"Where are your coaches?" asked the Signalman.

Thomas looked behind him. "Oh, no!" he cried.

Thomas returned to Knapford Station, where Sir Topham Hatt was trying to calm the unhappy passengers.

Thomas said he was very sorry.

"You still have a lot to learn, little Thomas," said Sir Topham Hatt sternly.

The passengers climbed aboard. This time, Thomas waited for the Guard to wave his flag before chuffing off.

The next day, Edward kindly offered
Thomas a chance to take his goods
train. He warned Thomas that trucks
sometimes played tricks on the engines.

"Don't be silly," Thomas said,
laughing.

"Be careful," Edward said seriously.

Things were going fine until Thomas reached a steep hill.

On the way down, the trucks sped up. Thomas was going so fast he nearly went off the track. At Maron Station, he stopped inches from the buffer.

"Why were you going so fast?" asked Sir Topham Hatt.

"Edward's trucks were pushing me," Thomas explained.

Sir Topham Hatt was cross with both engines and made them stay in the Yard.

Every day, Thomas worked very hard. He wanted
to be a Really Useful Engine.

One afternoon, he and Edward heard a train barreling toward the
Yard.

"Help!" James cried. "The trucks are pushing me!"

James sped through the Yard with smoke and sparks flying from his wheels.

"Use your brakes!" Thomas yelled as he raced after James.

"Can't! My brake blocks are on fire!" called James.

Thomas hurried to catch up with James. He was determined to help his friend.

Suddenly, James headed into a tight bend in the track and crashed right off the rails into a field. The Troublesome Trucks tipped over.

"I'll get help, James!" Thomas promised him.

Thomas raced back to Knapford Yard, right past Sir Topham Hatt, straight to the breakdown train.

"James has derailed and so have his trucks!" he called to Judy and Jerome.

"Crew up!" shouted Jerome. "Let's go, Judy!"

In no time, Judy and Jerome were ready to lift James back onto the track.

The broken trucks were sad and sorry now.

"I hope this will teach you a lesson!" scolded Thomas.

Sir Topham Hatt was pleased with Thomas. He asked him to take James to the Steamworks for repair.

The next day, James came back to the Yard with new brakes and a splendid new coat of shiny red paint.

That night, Sir Topham Hatt paid a surprise visit to the Sheds.
"Congratulations, Thomas," he said. "Due to your unselfish bravery,
you have shown yourself worthy of having your own Branch Line."

Thomas was proud and happy. Now he even had his very own
coaches, Annie and Clarabel.

Thomas the Tank Engine had become a Really Useful Engine at last!